Last Day Blues

Julie Danneberg • Illustrated by Judy Love

Published by Charlesbridge
85 Main Street
Watertown, MA 02472
(617) 926-0329
www.charlesbridge.com

Library of Congress Cataloging-in-Publication Data
Danneberg, Julie, 1958–
Last day blues / Julie Danneberg ; illustrated by Judy Love.
p. cm.
Summary: During the last week of school, the students in Mrs. Hartwell's class
try to come up with the perfect present for their teacher.
ISBN-13: 978-1-58089-046-5; ISBN-10: 1-58089-046-6 (reinforced for library use)
ISBN-13: 978-1-58089-104-2; ISBN-10: 1-58089-104-7 (softcover)
[1. Teachers—Fiction. 2. Schools—Fiction. 3. Gifts—Fiction.] I. Love, Judith DuFour, ill. II. Title.
PZ7.D2355 Las 2006
[E]—dc22   2005006011

Printed in China
(hc) 10 9 8 7 6 5 4 3 2 1
(sc) 10 9 8 7 6 5 4 3 2 1

Illustrations done in transparent dyes on Strathmore paper
Display type and text type set in Roger and Electra
Color separated, printed, and bound by Regent Publishing Services
Production supervision by Brian G. Walker
Designed by Diane M. Earley

On the Monday morning before the Friday that was the last day of school, Mrs. Hartwell took attendance. She sighed as she called out the last name, "I'm going to miss all of you," she said.

The kids nodded in agreement.
"I'm going to miss my friends,"
said Shannon.

"I'm going to miss Daisy," said Dan.

"I'm going to miss
chocolate milk and pizza
for lunch," said Joe.

Everyone felt a little blue thinking about the last day of school. Even Daisy.

That afternoon during recess, the students talked as they hung out on the jungle gym.

"Mrs. Hartwell said she's going to miss us," said Alexandra, swinging from a bar.

"We should get a present to cheer her up," said Eddie, hanging upside down by his knees.

But what could they get her?

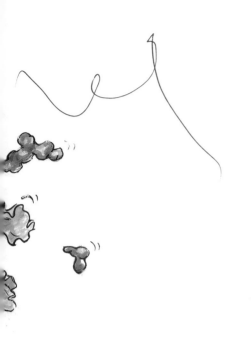

"I could give her the rest of my sandwich. It's my mom's baloney special," said Josh.

"Or a coffee cup."

"Or a new pen, the kind with feathers and beads."

The students thought and thought but couldn't come up with one single idea that they all agreed on.

"We'll think of something tomorrow," Eddie assured everyone as they lined up at the drinking fountain.

On the Tuesday before the Friday that was the last day of school, Mrs. Hartwell read the final page of their last read-aloud book.

"I'm going to miss circle time," said Mrs. Hartwell.

"I'm going to miss science," said Emily.

"I'm going to miss seeing Mrs. Hartwell wear her safety goggles during science," said Jack, giggling.

And so before they got too sad, Mrs. Hartwell put on her safety goggles one last time. Just for fun.

"We definitely need
to cheer Mrs. Hartwell
up," said Andy during recess
as he jumped out of a swing.
    "Any ideas about a present?"
Eddie asked.
    "Nope," they all answered back.

On the Wednesday before the Friday that was the last day of school, Mrs. Hartwell brought in her super-duper sugar cookies with extra frosting.

"I'm going to miss snack time, but I can't wait for barbecues by the pool," said Jack.

"I'm going to miss recess, but I can't wait to play hide-and-seek outside after dinner," said Alexandra.

I'm going fishing

I'm going to the

Beach

We're driving to

"I'll miss school, but I can't wait for summer vacation," said Josh.

The class discussed their summer plans and drowned their last day blues with another round of milk and sugar cookies.

"I don't know whether to be happy or sad today," Andy said the minute they all arrived at the jungle gym.

"Mrs. Hartwell is sad," said Olivia. "She probably doesn't want the year to end."

"While we're swimming, she'll be reading her old lesson plans," said Walker.

LESSON PLAN

"And while we're playing, she'll be trying to remember the fun times we had this year," said Dan.

And that's when an idea zipped, zapped, and zinged through Eddie's brain. "I know exactly what will cheer her up," Eddie said, jumping down from the jungle gym.

The class agreed it was perfect.

On the Thursday before the Friday that was the
last day of school, Eddie raised his hand right after
Mrs. Hartwell started language arts.

"We need some privacy, please," he said.

And so Mrs. Hartwell took down bulletin boards with her back to the class. She never even peeked. Well, only once.

On the morning of the Friday that was the Friday
that was the last day of school, the students dashed
into the classroom.

They snapped open the shades for the very last time.
They did their chores for the very last time.
They fed Daisy for the very last time.
And as soon as the bell rang, they couldn't wait for
Mrs. Hartwell to see her present for the very first time.

The last day of school makes us so blue.

We'll miss recess and pizza and reading, too.

We'll miss Daisy and cookies and friendship true,

Snack time and science and learning new.

We'll miss spelling bees for our test review

And groundhogs that play Peek-a-boo.

The year's been great, a big WAHOO!

There are many things to miss — it's true.

But mostly what we'll miss

is YOU!

Joe

Josh

Alexandra — everyone is a Teacher

Jack

Margaret

Carol

A B C

Carl

Eddie ♥ Most

Sam

You're #1

Janice

Olivia

Shannon

Zack

Walker

Maria

Daniel

Eddie

F.D.

Andy

Later on during recess, Eddie said, "I think Mrs. Hartwell liked her present."

"I just hope it helps," Margaret said.

"Poor Mrs. Hartwell," they all said sadly as they pictured their final good-bye. "Teachers must hate the last day of school."

And then it was time. The bell rang.

"Good-bye," the students called as they rushed out the door.

"Good-bye," Mrs. Hartwell called after them.

And then she returned to her empty classroom. "It's just you and me, Daisy," she said. "I'm sure going to miss them this summer . . .

. . . but I can't wait for vacation!"